A Gronking to Remember 2: Chad Goes Deep in the Neutral Zone

Book Two in the Rob Gronkowski Erotica Series

LACEY NOONAN

ISBN: 1507785887
ISBN-13: 978-1507785881

Disclaimer

This is a work of fiction and is not intended maliciously. Any resemblance to actual persons, living or dead, or actual events, except in cases when public figures are being satirized, is purely coincidental.

A Gronking to Remember 2: Chad Goes Deep in the Neutral Zone by Lacey Noonan is a work of satire and is in no way endorsed by the National Football League, The New England Patriots, Robert Gronkowski or any of his business entities.

CONTENTS

Prologue

Chad, my sweet Chad... Why did you do it? What did you see in me?

You broke me down. You built me up. You taught me everything. You showed me there is no such thing as that multi-fisted monstrous orgasm, that chandelier of nuclear light, that five man rush to the senses, without a foundation of fundamentals. If you're bringing the house, you need a foundation... You taught me that, Coach Chad.

Oh, but Chad, have you really taught me everything you know or do you hold back, my Chadmeister General, my Chadhesive Strip, my Chadirondack Chair, my John Quincy Chadams? And why do I hate you so? I hate that I hate you, still. For there is always a kind of resentment between student and teacher. You showed me how wrong I was, how silly and ignorant. You forged me in the crucible of your psyche, like a hot burning stove; you showed me how little I knew, like those trapped in Plato's Cave enamored by dancing shadows on the wall.

But you know that I could never hate you for long, Chad, and I hate you for knowing it. Because deep down, I know you showed me who I was really meant to be.

As I wander alone this dark Neutral Zone, chasing shadows like TLC chasing waterfalls, know that you will always be a part of me. Godspeed, this full-grown woman will never forget you.

Aye-aye, carry on, my sweet Chadmiral!

CHAPTER I
Sorry If I'm Making You Uncomfortable

"I'll never forget the first time I saw Gronk spike a football," I said into the microphone and looked out over the crowd.

Goosebumps rippled to life along the back of my neck like wind on water. The lady downstairs jiggled with butterflies. I felt hot. And I *was* hot. I knew I was the shit, but I was still nervous. The place was packed and all eyes were on me. "It changed my life forever..." I whispered into the mic with emotional gravitas.

What was I doing?

A reading—this was my thang-thang now. Press junkets. PR conjuring. Readings and Q&A's. It had been a nonstop whirlwind of reporters prodding me for anecdotes and myth-deflating secrets ever since I'd published my memoir: *A Gronking to Remember;*

and then my chapbook of poetry: *Wife Spiked By Life*.

The tour was exhausting. Dan and I had criss-crossed the country together, seeing the sights, playing hide the salami in hotel rooms and the odd public park. Our love blossomed, bloomed and boomed, born-again on the field of battle (Gillette Stadium). It was like a second honeymoon, really. It was fun, but I was itching for it to be over with.

And now here we were, at the last reading, happy to be heading home. I turned the pages and recited the words I had recited for weeks now. As far as grand finales went it was highly baller: A reading at the 92nd Street Y in Manhattan, hosted by NPR's Terry Gross, who, as it turned out, was a rabid NFL fan.

Needless to say, I was psyched. Terry *motherfucking* Gross. The Queen Tee herself. Lady Tee. Finally! Someone intellectual who I could talk to about the cerebral aspects of what I'd gone through and not all the dumb hero worship and the salacious aspects of the big honking, bonking Gronking. Yes, psyched was the word—psyched until, that is, she started asking me questions…

I finished reading and took my seat between Dan (he was a part of this too after all, my partner in exhibitionist games) and Terry, who both wore Cheshire cat grins, smiling at me as I crossed the stage amid the applause washing in from the auditorium.

"Thanks, Leigh, that was great," Terry said. "*Yuge*."

Dan leaned over and kissed me on the cheek.

"So, Leigh, what is *with* you and Rob Gronkowski?" Terry was no nonsense—jumped straight into the questions.

"Well, I mean—"

"God, that spike, right?" Terry said. "Tell us about *dat spike doe*," she said and there was a titterous laughter throughout the auditorium. I was getting the unpleasant feeling Terry was making fun of me.

"Oh. You know. Like I said in the book. You know. It was amazing... It's kind of hard to talk about. You know."

"Hmm. Yeah. So when the ball exploded in your butthole, did you know you were going to have an orgasm and if—"

"But it really didn't land in my... um, my butthole," I cut in. "Gronk's gronk landed somewhere else entirely... gronked not just near or even *in* my butt, but in my butt of butts. The inner butt. A mystical place, like a neutral zone, the mystical neutral butt, like the inner light that we have in all of us."

"Oh, okaaaay," Terry said and laughed. "So do you consider what you have to be a perversion?" she then asked, uncharacteristically brusque. "What do you call it? Foot-butt-ball-hole-philia?"

I was shocked. The very brusqueness! I couldn't speak.

"What about... Gronkosexuality?" she continued.

"I— I— I... What I have?" I finally stammered. I bit my lip and squeezed my knees. I wasn't ready for this kind of question from Terry. It was "Gotcha! Media" at its most trenchant.

"To be sexually satisfied by a football, spiked in the butt of butts by a *yuge* football player," Terry continued. "It's weird, right?"

"It's *not* a perversion!" I squawked.

"Sorry if I'm making you uncomfortable. Usually I preface a question like that with a warning, like, if this is too personal a question, feel free to not answer it, something like that."

"I mean, it was just such a personal thing. It's hard to talk about sex in public for me. I'm still an old New England girl at heart, maybe puritan," I said. There was some light clapping throughout the auditorium. A whistle of approval. Or was that a catcall?

"Why not show us then?" Terry said.

"I'm not sure what you—"

"I think I'd be remiss in my journalistic duties if I didn't ask you if you could spike a football in my booty," Terry said to me, then looked out to the audience and said, "Wouldn't that be *so* cool if we could witness it live?"

Unbelievable!

Of course, since "The Gronking to Remember" a few months earlier, random people would come up to me on the street and ask me to spike a football into their ass, or ask Dan and I to act it out if we were together. (You'd be surprised at just how many people walked around with footballs these days. It was an epidemic. A pandemic of epic proportions.)

More often than not I accepted at first, but quickly got weirded out by the requests.

I was starting to understand celebrity. Suddenly everything you worked so hard for isn't yours any more. You work and work, and then when you reach that pinnacle it becomes everyone else's. They see themselves in you, and in America, where fantasy and hope play such a huge part of peoples' lives, there's nothing you can do—you've got to give it away or it will eat you alive. Something so personal and personality-forming as the episode out on the field at Gillette stadium—rich, dark, and deep down in the mud of my person—was suddenly not my own. After a while I was fine to let it go. I had to. You hold on to this thing that people are clawing at and their claws tear into you and finally you have to let it go because they'll claw you to death in the mix.

But that was normal, non-famous people. You don't expect that kind of shit from other celebrities!

Needless to say, coming from Terry Gross, star of the NPR talk show *Fresh Air*, the "ball in the butt" request was a huge—*yuge*—letdown.

"Sorry, Terry," I said. "There's no way. I don't do that—I mean, I can't. There's too much wrapped up in it. Too much love."

Terry smiled wider and pulled out a large brown football from behind her chair. "Pwetty PWEASE???" she said.

I shook my head.

There were cheers from the audience. Now there were definite calls of the cat, I heard. Boston and New England fans were notorious for traveling everywhere to see their teams. Did that extend to memoir readings too?

I was confounded. Vexed and hexed. I looked over to Dan. He was looking about as put upon as I was. But he leaned over and whispered in my ear. "Come on, Leigh. This'll be great publicity. It'll helps sales. You got to," he said.

The crowd was getting loud and intense. I felt like I was about to cry. Out of the corner of my eye I could see Terry waving the ball back and forth. I beseeched Dan with pleading tears in my eyes. "Please," I mouthed. "Please, let's just go," I said. "Please!"

The crowd is getting ugly now. Terry is nearly foaming at the mouth like some kind of Beatlemania fan, except not for four Mop Tops but for getting spiked in the butt with an inflated bag of wind. It's like we're at an actual game—a game, a riot, anything nastypants.

Finally, Dan saves the day.

"I'll do it," Dan says, standing up. He grabs the ball from Terry's hand. "I'll do it!" he says again, and the audience cheers. "Just so we can get the hell out of here."

"That would be yuge," Terry says. "Amazing."

Moving quickly, Terry gets down on all fours on the stage. Her butt is high in the air, wobbling on thin legs, wiggling back and forth like a cat ready to pounce.

My mind would not have believed what my eyes were seeing if my mouth had tried to describe it first.

Terry has on tight, tan slacks. You can see the contours of her buttocks, and—dear God—was that the lower digits of a certain long-necked ungulate mammal? *Oh God, oh Lord, Oh sweet lordly God*, I think to myself.

Tears stream down my face under the stage lights. Though the humiliation I would suffer in the next few days made all else pale in comparison, as I watch Terry on the stage I quail for the humiliation of it all. What had we become? Humanity, I mean. I know it was kinda crazy what happened at Gillette Stadium, when Dan flung me out under the Gronkaboy's powerful jammer but it was still very personal and I didn't think it was that funny. It was about love.

Good God, this is my life now, I think. *Sweet, peaceful loom, tender yarn, wise and noble knitting needles, I am coming. I am coming home for you. Coming home for silence, for peace from all this deafening pop-culture riot.*

"Thank you," Terry mouths, looking from me to Dan, then back to me. "Thank you."

Dan pulls the football back and lets if fly.

It was a wobbler, but it found the zone place.

CHAPTER II
Sedanimal

The sedan barreled east through the rain and the darkness on CT-15.

Dan reached out and squeezed my hand. I looked at him. There was adoration in his eyes, a Franklin Stove of love in each socket that should have melted me down to margarine, but I was still shaken from the sordid stage drama.

"Why did you think that was okay, Dan?"

"Because it will help us sell books, Leigh. You know that. We need to make money, girl."

"We have enough money by now, don't we?"

Dan sighed equivocally and looked out at the landscape whizzing past. Rain was jizzing across the window in see-through rivulets. NPR had splurged on a car service for us to get home. There was a barrier between us and the driver. Maybe because of this, hubby was feeling liberal with his intimacy.

Dan suddenly got real close and coddled me with a warm arm and said: "Chad and Andrea are having that welcome back thing tonight."

"Are you serious?"

"I know, I know…"

"Come on, Dan. I'm tired. I'm exhausted. I just wanna go home and sink into the tub and let Calgon take me away for a million forevers."

"I'm sorry, sugar plum. You know I love you." Dan nuzzled up to me and kissed my neck. "Come on. You know it'll be good for you. Take your mind off things. A big, empty house is only going to depress us."

I turned and for a brief second I saw Gronk in the reflection of the window, a fleeting glimpse of an ephemeral meaty brow. This had been happening a lot lately, naturally. Gronk had infused my life. He was like a perfume that traveled with me everywhere. He was the specter haunting my Europe. I'd hitched my wagon to the shooting star of Gronk and it had taken me for a ride wilder than any ride I'd ever been on. Life was a Gronkachusetts Turnpike—even on the Merritt Parkway—and suddenly I had an EZ Pass.

I sighed. I really wanted to get home, but Dan had honestly come through for me on the stage with Terry, so I felt like I owed him one.

"Um, which one is Chad again?" I asked.

"You remember. The Pats fan who sits by the window. The one I'm—I *was*—always having to punch in the dick 'cause he starts with me about the Jets and tries to punch me in the dick about it."

"But that's all over, right?"

"Oh yeah. 'Course.'"

"Fine," I said. "We can go. But only for an hour, okay?"

"Good girl." Reaching up under my jacket, he squeezed one of my titties, tweaking the nipple like an inquisitor manqué. I inhaled in surprise.

"What are you—"

"Oh, nothing…"

"The driver…"

"Is watching the road."

"Hmm."

"But you need to watch this choad." Dan grabbed my hand, pulled it down to his crotch, to the front of his Wranglers.

"Well, well, well… what do we have here?" I said, my voice low so the driver wouldn't hear through the partition. I wasn't sure if I was willing to *do it* in a car, but I couldn't stop myself from conforming my hand to the lovely shape I touched. A lovely tube, harder than hard, ensconced in durable and fashionably distressed Wranglers like an iron fist in a velvet glove.

"I liked being out there with you. Giving it good like that, Leigh. It turned me on."

"Why, thank you, Mr. Man," I whispered in my best sultry-Suzanne-Sugarbaker voice.

"You're a sexy woman. That is just plain obvious to anyone with eyes. You really know how to take a ball."

"Mmm… Should I do my job?" I asked.

"Do your job. It is imperative that you do so."

I unzipped Dan's pants and unleashed the dragon.

It was as thick and hard as a Franklin Stove.

"I do declare," I sultrified. My mouth watered and I rubbed my legs together like a cricket. How naughty—the driver right there, the romantic rain, the Merritt Parkway whizzing and jizzing past.

About twenty minutes later, if you were on Route 15 in Connecticut on the way to I-84, just under the bridge with the ornate Art Deco spider web, you would have seen what looked like a very small jellyfish launch from the cracked window of a midsized black sedan, only to go sailing elegantly into the rainy and headlight-lit night like a Hail Mary, and you would have been not incorrect to assume that it was a prophylactic, ribbed and lubricated for her pleasure.

CHAPTER III

Hitting the Red Margs Hard

The door was flung open like the front of a Franklin Stove, throwing its warmth and welcoming light on the dark, wet night wetting us.

Chad stood there in a halo of light, beaming. His wife Andrea was just over his shoulder.

"Look Leigh, when you get sick of Dan," Chad said, "I just want you to know I'd leave Andrea in heartbeat."

There was a strained laugh over Chad's shoulder, and Andrea's face, which already had small, pinched features, pinched even further.

Dan and I walked into the vestibule and shook off the cold and damp. The sounds of an idiotic Connecticut gathering tinkled and cranked behind our hosts in the house. Chad continued, "I mean, it's not every day you're in the same room as the number one

Gronkowski fan in the world!"

"Well, I wouldn't say—"

"And she's married to a *fucking Jets* fan!" Chad shouted and shook his hands in faux consternation in front of his face. His voice echoed up in the faux rafters of their McMansion.

"C'mon Chad, you know I've moved on from the Jets…" Dan said placatingly.

"God dammit, do I get hard just thinking about Gronk!" Chad shouted. Another pinched laugh matriculated over his shoulder.

"Hmmm. What's that you're drinking there, duder?" Dan said, trying to change the subject. I looked and realized Chad was already pretty drunk, holding a big red drink in his hand, one of those elongated plastic Mardis Gras cups. "Pre-gaming without us? What the eff, buddy?"

Chad laughed and the guys went in towards the party. Bros 4 Lyfe.

"Hey you!" Andrea shouted in my face, as if I'd just walked in and a Vince Wilfork-sized avalanche of awkwardness hadn't just happened right in her very own McVestibule. Andrea worked in marketing, so always had multiple layers of bullshit going at once. Overly-and-falsely-effusive before I became famous (or infamous), Andrea always greeted me now with barely-hidden disgust. "How was the little tour? Awful, I bet! I bet you're glad to go back to your cute sewing and stuff."

Rather than answer I just smiled, took her arm and walked in towards the party.

So if our entrance was pretty much 1.21 Jigawatts

of awkwardsauce, our eventual exit was a resounding 1.22…

About a half an hour later, the effulgent red drinks, which I found out the hard way were potent margaritas, got the better of me and I went upstairs to tinkle.

I went into their bathroom, about eight sizes too big. *Did they have dance rehearsals in here?* I thought to myself as I dropped my pants and sat on the toilet.

Suddenly, a voice filled the bathroom.

"He's using you!"

I screamed and jumped up from the pot.

"I'm serious, Leigh. He's using you," came the voice again, this time with laughter. I realized in an instant it was Chad. I heard a noise in the shower. He was in there, behind the curtain.

"What the fuck, Chad! How did you get in here?"

"Are you… *decent* again, if I—?"

"What the fuck?" I yelled and ran for the door, pulling up my underpants and slacks on the way. I felt so incredibly exposed.

My hand was on the knob when Chad's meaty paw came shooting out from behind the curtain, covering mine.

"Ah!" I screamed and pulled my hand away.

"Search out your heart, Leigh. You know I'm right."

"What the fuck are you—?" I said. And when Chad pulled his hand away to open the curtain, I opened the bathroom door as fast as I could and went out into the hall.

Somehow Chad was there before I was. His body

blurred by mine and now stood between me and the stairs leading back down to the party.

"Darkness is coming. The truth shall set you free."

"What the *literal* fuck is wrong with you?" I whisper-snorted.

Chad wobbled in place. He'd obviously been hitting the red margs hard. He licked his dry lips. His eyes rolled around, taking pit stops all over my body before finally settling, gentlemanly, on my eyes. I'd forgotten what dealing with dumbass drunks was like. Dan had gone cold-turkey like Leonardo DiCaprio in the *Basketball Diaries* over the three weeks we spent in the holding cell at Gillette Stadium awaiting trial, and he never went back.

"You know he's using you, Leigh."

"Who?"

"Dan. Danimal is," Chad said, then began the long process unfurling a wide, knowing grin across his lower face. He took a step closer to me.

"Um, okay? Using me for what?" I said and stepped back.

"So you know Danimal doesn't give a shit about the Patriots, right—how he's straight up no chaser lying if he says he's changed teams, no more Jetty Jets?"

"Look Chad, I don't really care about that..." I said and smiled, trying to stay positive. I wasn't exactly on full-alert yet, though if I'd known what was going to happen later, I should have yanked the ugly brown Pier One lamp off the table next to us and smashed it across Chad's big, fat glabella. "Chad, you're drunk…"

"So what. Your Dan's a no-good Jets fan, girl. He's dangerous. He's a liar, he's lying to you if he's saying he's changed. I'm sorry to break the truth to you like this. Look, if you ever want to get together and talk football, I'm your man, right? Drop that zero and get with this hero, Leigh. Patriots for life. *New England* Patriots."

"Actually, Dan's been pretty good with the—"

"Leigh—fucking Danimal—listen! I'm serious. Before it's too late. Okay? I mean, The Gronking to Remember, out on the touchdown thing, that was *amazing*. Every man, woman and child's fantasy… Touch the hero… Hero touching is what we live for. I mean, Belichick is… Brady is a god too around this house. Look, you wanna come check out my man cave? I have like so much Pats gear you wouldn't believe. Chadmiral's Quarters, I call it. You'd love it, I'm serious…"

His waterfall of nonsense stopped on a dime. It was like someone had unplugged a super-loud rock band right in the middle of their loudest song: the silence was deafening.

I just shook my head.

"Leigh, can I say something?"

"If it isn't annoying."

"Me too," he said, oddly, and paused a beat. "I think about you all the time," he unleashed with emotion and perspiration. "Run away with me. Oh, run away with me, Leigh! Let's go to an island together and watch Patriot games."

"*Patriot Games?* That movie sucked. Mel Gibson?

Blech!"

Chad looked confused; what I said was a joke, but he was taking it seriously. He frowned. I really needed to get back downstairs before this got weird.

But then the move was made.

Chad grabbed me. Before I knew what was going on, his hands were palpitating on my upper arms like two blood pressure gauges.

"Chad, no," I said quietly but firmly.

"Chad, yes," Chad said and leaned in closer.

His smell was in my personal space now: margarita and sweat mixed with a manly, leather kind of odor.

Chad pulled me close. He opened his mouth. Was he going to eat my nose? I scrunched up my face harder than Andrea's face, squeezing my whole body in defense as if to make myself invisible, impenetrable to this poisonous assault.

Chad's tongue lathered my cheek like a sloppy elephant schnozzle.

"Only I understand you," he breathed hotly. His meaty paws were on my body, running all over me like a teen wind puppet out of control. He cupped a tit. Squeezed a cheek. "I wanna fuck you like a Danimal."

A voice suddenly rang out extremely loud and incredibly close. "Chad! The *fuck*, man!" It was Dan, thank God, on the staircase just below us. "What. The. Fuck. Man."

Dan stormed up the remaining stairs and shoved Chad against the wall. The lamp rattled in place on the table. I scampered away, I could feel the approach of violence on the wind, like a Native American listening to a train track.

Downstairs the party was in full swing. Adults and near-adults were talking loudly. Hootie and the Blowfish played on the stereo. A 90's Spotify mix spit out songs along a calculating algorithm, unaware it calculated ironically. No one seemed to be aware of what was going on just up on the landing upstairs. I came into the room shaking, nerves vibrating at 100 mph.

Andrea was sitting on the arm of a couch with a marg in her hand and dumbass squint on her face. I practically ran up to her. She sneered at me, "Oh hai, Leigh-Leigh. You drop a deuce? You were up there long—"

"*Goddamit*, Andrea, *listen* for once in your fucking—"

Andrea's gaze shifted over my shoulder and I spun around.

The two men came down the stairs, arms around each other's shoulders. They were smiling and babbling drunkenly. Dan had gotten drunk too, I realized. This was a revelation. Each guy wielded a full, tall, red, strong, effulgent margarita.

I posted up in front of them. "What *the* hell?"

"Chad and I worked it out."

"Oh, wow, you worked it out. Fucking *great*." I was peeved. Typical male crapola. My feelings weren't part of the equation. I was a commodity. "Okay," I said deep into Dan's eyeballs, "Home now."

"Leigh, come ahhhhhhhhhhhhhhhhhhnnnnnn…" Chad said.

"Yeahhhhhhhhhhhhhhhhh…" Dan drawled for

ten years.

"...nnnnnnnnnnnnnn—" Chad continued.

"Now!" I said through clenched teeth.

"But I'm derrrnk, wen need t'call a cur."

"The NPR car is still waiting out in the fucking driveway you fucking drunk fuck. Let's *go*."

I didn't wait for an answer. I went to the foyer, found my coat and walked out into the night, slamming the door loudly behind me, my heart boiling like a pot of whale blubber in a Franklin Stove.

Dan eventually followed, after fifteen minutes and probably twice as many margs. He was drunker than I'd ever seen him. He fell into the car and immediately fell asleep. We made it home and the driver helped me carry Dan inside. I tried to tip the driver but he said, "No thanks, ma'am, it's all been paid for by Terry Gross and the NPR," and with a tip of the toque he evaporated the sleek black sedan into the gothic black night of Connecticut.

I wandered around our house—so many thoughts, so many wild and divergent thoughts filled my head. I felt filled-up, yet somehow incomplete at the same time. What was I missing? It wasn't until a couple hours later that I figured out what it was…

My head had just kissed the pillow when I realized I hadn't laid eyes on my sewing room since getting back. I really missed my Leclercs, the aforementioned *Voyageur* as well as the giant *Nilus II 8s Countermarch*, a veritable Snuffleupagus I'd picked up after the first royalty checks from YouTube had come in, and my assortment of fine yarns and needles. *Did they miss me too?* I wondered. The ensuing fruitless, suppurating argument with Dan had eaten up the rest of the night and I was exhausted. I was loath to get up. Sleep was but a shorthair away.

"Screw it," I whispered and got up out of bed. I wish I hadn't. I wish I'd stayed safely in bed under the covers next to Daniel, my hubby, my partner, my protector, my lover, my Danny Boy, my Danimal.

I walked through the sleeping house, my way softly lit by the green and red standby lights of our myriad electronic bric-a-brac. I went through the kitchen and was just about to go into the sewing room. Suddenly, I was being looked at. There was a face.

A face of pure evil stepped from the shadows!

My lungs clenched up—I tried to scream but couldn't. The face's materialization was so frightening and so unexpected, my lungs just sucked and sucked in air and I nearly passed out. And before I could finally scream out for help, the rag doused with chloroform was on my mouth and the black hood was over my head.

I was just able to make out the face before everything went black. There was evil in its eyes. And mischief.

All went dark and the evil face followed me into my blackened dreams…

CHAPTER IV
Where the Fuck Am I?

I came to.

In that brief moment before I opened my eyes, I was safe. My consciousness awoke and I was the same old Leigh, safe and snug next to Dan in our bed, stretching in the lilting darkness before I opened my eyes.

Then I opened my eyes and gazed upon a true darkness.

"WHERE THE FUCK AM I!?" I shouted, trying to take in the very confusing place I found myself—my eyes were still blurry, I was groggy, and there were a million clashing colors.

Or at least *WHERE THE FUCK AM I!?* was what I wanted to shout. What I really shouted was more like, "Mmf mm mmf m mmm," because there was a ball gag in my mouth.

There was something else too. I was restrained at the ankles and wrists.

With horror I looked down at my body. I tried not to panic, but panic was everywhere.

Memories came flying back. The night before…

The walk to the sewing room. The evil and mischievous face in the dark. The chloroform. The capturing. Was I dreaming? No. I wasn't dreaming. This was worse than a nightmare. This was real.

Motherfucking *real*.

Cold... A chill ran its fingers over my bare skin, tickled goosebumps to life. At some point while I was passed out, someone had removed my pajamas. They were nowhere to be found. My bra and panties were all that remained to cover my quivering flesh. My thighs, my stomach, my shoulders were vulnerable and presentable. Even what was *under* my panties and bra were vulnerable... I trembled to think how very unprotective a ladies underthings truly were. A coy gesture of protection. What the fuck was wrong with me the night before that hadn't I worn battle armor to bed?

It really didn't matter though. *I'm getting the fuck out of here*! I yelled (in my mind).

I pulled at my restraints—shook them violently—but they were incredibly tight. It was no use. I couldn't move. I was strapped down on a huge, thick, comfortable chair. Wait. This was strange—why a comfortable chair? It was very puffy and soft. My arms were up over my head chained together and my legs were spread apart over the plush armrests.

And then I began to take in my surroundings and I began to recognize more and more things.

Everywhere—and I mean everywhere—were NFL souvenirs, bric-a-brac, gewgaws and mementos, mixed in with sex dungeon type stuff—toys or weapons— toys that looked like weapons and vice versa.

To my right was a bar. There were neon Bud Light signs, taps, everything. On the wall directly in front of me there was a flatscreen TV that must have been fifteen feet wide.

It was almost too much to take in. It was all over the walls, the ceiling—even all over the floor: signed NFL jerseys, an assortment of whips, signed footballs behind glass, an assortment of dildos, signed framed photographs of football players, an assortment of lubricants, a signed trainer's bench and a massage bench with strategically located holes and handcuffs draped on it.

The room was like a Hard Rock Café, except a fucked up, warped-fantasy-commingling of pro sports and pervy sex.

And then with a jolt of electric horror jelly I realized that there was a *ton* of my needlework mixed in throughout the various artifacts. There was an embroidered pillow of Bill Belichick in a hood next to a large red buttplug. And there was a quilt of Gronkowski pictured in the middle of gronking the ball hanging like a tapestry next to the largest and most nasty looking cat o' nine tails I'd ever seen. I'd only made the one Gronk quilt and sold it on etsy for $3,800. I wracked my brain for who had bought it, but couldn't remember. After a while, Dan handled the shipping because I couldn't keep up with the orders.

Who? Who had done this to me?

Though the question echoed in my head like a PA announcement at a stadium for what seemed like an eternity, I didn't have long to wait to find out.

There were noises behind me. Shuffling, banging, scraping.

Oh God, Oh God, Oh God... Someone was coming. I tried to stretch my neck around to see but I was tied down too tight.

I heard a door open and close. A nasty puff of freezing cold wind wafted into the room and chilled me to my core.

The door closed and a man entered the room. He came around and stood before me. He was naked except for a silver football helmet and a jock strap. And lodged under his crooked elbow, a football.

"Well, look who's finally up," he said. "Are you ready to get down to business? Welcome to Chadmiral's Quarters."

It was Chad.

WTF!!!!!!!!!!!!!!!!!!!!!!!!!!!!!!!!!!!!!!

CHAPTER V
Welcome to Chadmiral's Quarters

"Mmf mmf mmf!" I mmfed.

"I know, I know!" Chad exclaimed, waving his hand around as if he wanted me take it all in: his playroom for the deranged fan. "Pretty neat, huh?" He let fly with one of his big smiles.

"Mmf mmmmf mmmmff!"

"I know, I can't believe you're finally here either!"

"Mm mmm!"

"It'll be *so good* to *finally* get down to business now that we can be *alone.*"

"Mmf mmmmmmf!"

"Sorry, sugar pie, what?"

"Mmf mmmmmmf!"

"Sorry, I can't quite make out what you're saying." Chad walked up to me and placed the ball he was carrying between my legs. It was ice cold and sent snaky shivers up my thighs into my darling hips. I was afraid; he was so close and… nude. I'd assumed he was fat and blobby like Dan's other friends, but pretty much naked in front of me, I had to admit—mainly with utmost, crawling fear—that Chad was ripped. He had bulging muscles and a flat stomach, with abs falling down to a low-slung jock, vainly covering his manhood. His jaw was strong, he had dark hair and dark features. He untied the ball gag. A waterfall of saliva poured out of my mouth. "There. Now what were—?"

I let out a blood-curdling scream: "Heeeeeeelp! Helllllllllllllp!" I screamed. I screamed so loud flashes of light blinded my vision. "Dan! Dan! Dan! Helllllppppppplllllppppp!" I screamed for ice cream.

Chad frowned and tried to put the ball gag back in. I went full rabid dog: I chomped at his hands, shook my head back and forth, screamed, frothed at the mouth.

After a few moments Chad must have gotten sick of my shenanigans. He took my right nipple tightly between his fingers and twisted, torturing it. Pain rectified me, as if the nip were attached by a long cord to my vital organs.

I yelped in agony. My mouth was only open for less than a second, but it was all he needed. The gag was back in my mouth before I knew it. And all I had to show for my glorious rebellion was a stinging nipple.

Chad took a step back and regarded me with a look a teacher might give a misbehaving first grader. "I was really hoping we could get along, Leigh. I really was," he said and walked over to the wall. The sundry gewgaws shone in the neon Bud Light light—the NFL party favors and the nasty sex toys. I watched his taut, bare buttocks framed in the off-white straps of his jock shimmy back and forth as he ran his hands idly over the Heisman trophy, over the dangling Ben Wa miscellany, over a bust of Victor Kiam, over a very-pointy-and-very-painful-looking fire poker.

"I was really hoping we could work together, Leigh. I mean, we're both such huge fans of the Patriots. Seemed like a match made in heaven."

"Mmmf."

"True. Very true."

"Mmmmmmm."

"Oh, that's such a very *sweet* thing to say, saying we're made for each other. Oh, my stars and garters." And he reached down and snapped the strap on his left cheek.

"Mm mm mm mm mm mm mm mm mmm mm mf mf mmmmmmm."

"Okay, if you think so. If you think you need a little *correcting* to get into the swing of things—how things are going to go. That's a swell idea."

"MMMMM!"

Chad lifted the long poker from the wall and hoisted it in his hands, as if testing the weight. It was black, as black as a cast-iron Franklin Stove, and looked like something Queequeg might hurl at a sperm whale.

I trembled. I began to cry. Oh God, how did this happen? Why was I so stupid to not have seen it before—that this Chad character was a psycho, a fan beyond the brink of sanity? The bathroom incident… His protestations of love… The psycho doth protest too much…

Chad shimmied over from the wall to the chair. Standing before me, he reached the poker out and slowly, ever so tender and slowly, as I began to scream into my ball gag, run it up the inside of my right arm.

I was nearly peeing myself with fright, like the Buffalo Bills must do whenever they have to play at Gillette Stadium.

The head of the poker was deadly sharp. It felt like a knife, though he was just teasing me with it so far. Chad ran it up my arm and then down to my neck. He drifted it across my shoulder blades and then circled my breasts with it. He then trailed it down my stomach and playfully ran the point along my inner thighs. And then he began to focus on my…

The poker found the cold football between my legs. Chad quickly pressed the head into the ball and…

POW!

The ball exploded! It popped right between my legs.

My throat went raw and hot. I screamed into my gag. I felt a dribble of pee release, soft and hot, below.

I began to writhe around to get away from the poker, my eyes wide with shock and terror.

"That's a good girl, yesssss. Fight it, fight it," he said, as he began to chase my chin around with the poker, "It shows you have fight. And what do you need to do to win when the chips are down, you're down at the end of the fourth quarter?"

"Mmf!"

"That's right! Fight, fight, fight!" Chad laughed with joy. It was a boring, insurance salesman kind of laugh that took on a cast of insanity considering the circumstances. His teeth shown bright white in the darkness of his football helmet—obviously a Patriots helmet.

For some reason pleased with the answer he imagined I'd given him, Chad returned the ancient weapon to the wall of knickknacks.

"Now, let's see," he drawled. "Now for some *real* fun."

Oh God, now what? I thought. *What's coming off the wall of horrors to torment me now?*

He opened a little hutch and pulled out something I couldn't immediately see.

Then, a second later, I saw it.

It looked like a Taser, some kind of electrical torture device. (I wasn't too up on the hot new sado-machines.) I had a very, very low tolerance for pain and knew that whatever this thing could dish out, I couldn't dish in.

As my legs shook and my whole body quivered with fear like a jello mold on a table as a fat dude walks by it, my one real hope was that I knew the second something painful happened to me that I would pass out, and with the agony of the doomed, I hoped that maybe the jolt of anti-jiggling-ribbon-joy would kill me altogether and I wouldn't have to suffer whatever sick, twisted indignities this sick fuck Chad had in store for me.

But then Chad got loose with his "device" and it was far worse and far weirder than I'd imagined.

CHAPTER VI
I Know What You Want

Chad removed my gag again. With strange, focused tenderness, he unlatched it from behind and deslurped the ball from between my lips. I wasn't stupid enough to scream out this time, just looked at him with fire and ire in my eyes and stretched my jaw to alleviate the soreness of the gag, which I saw, unbelievably, had the retro Pat Patriot logo on it. Was there an inch on this godforsaken earth not trammeled by the product placement?

"Feeling better?" he asked.

I did not answer.

"Oh come, come. That's no way to be," he said, then patted me on the cheek with one hand and ominously raised the electric thingie in the other.

"I—I, I don't know!" I tried not to yell. My throat was hoarse and dry.

"Do you need anything? Are you comfortable?"

"W-w-what are you going to do to me?" I said. Tears welled up; I began to cry.

"Come, come. Surely you must be thirsty or hungry by now."

I didn't answer. I couldn't answer. Helpless sobs rocked my chest. My bosom went up and down. I was practically naked and totally defenseless.

Then Chad raised the device up to me and I screamed.

He shushed me lightly, then pressed a button on it and the huge puffy brown chair beneath me began to move.

Now I really screamed.

Chad stepped back and smiled, two dimples materializing in his cheeks—the fucking psycho.

I watched with horror as this long metal tube rose up to my right. "Oh God Oh God Oh God!"

"Chill, Leigh," dimpled Chad chided.

The tube rose up like a snake and spun its head around, pointing directly at me. Then it made for my mouth, which I clamped shut. But before I knew what was going on, Chad pressed another button and the snake head squirted me in the face. It was water.

"Drinketh, m'lady."

I didn't realize how thirsty I was until the water hit my face. I opened and let the snake shoot its life-sustaining venom into my mouth. I drank heartily. After five gulps I realized it was Bud Light—basically water—sportsman's drink of the universe.

"Custom made," Chad said proudly. "A *real* man's Man Cave should have one of these."

"Look, Chad, what is all this? Why are you doing this?" I said quickly.

"What do you mean?"

"Why am I here? Why did you do this? Why am I here?"

"Only because I know what you like. I know what Dan doesn't like."

"That doesn't make any... Respectfully, Chad, respectfully, with utmost respect I ask that you let me go. Please. *Please*. I can pay you whatever you want."

"Oh, you'll be paying me what I want," he said with a lascivious sneer, "You'll be paying, and you'll be wanting to pay it."

"W-w-what does that mean?" I began to quiver again, my bones rattled in my body like someone shaking a quiver full of arrows.

"Look, it's simple. You're here because you need to be here. You were meant to be here. Dan doesn't give a shit about the *real you*. I know your wittle Dan-imal's brainwashed you. Dan doesn't love you like I love you. I can give you what you want."

"W-w-what do I want?"

"Gronk!"

I screamed as Chad raised the electronic device again. But he did not use it to squirt me down. He pointed it at the TV and the giant TV came to life.

On the screen was a football game. A Patriots game, and it was paused.

"Now, Leigh, I know how much watching Gronk turns you on, so I've compiled what I think are the *absolute hottest* Gronk moments *ever*. You're seriously going to be sore after I'm done with you. You can't even imagine *how* many times I *'watched'* this mix tape, wink, wink."

"No, please! Why!? You monster! You know what watching Gronk does to me! You can't! You can't! You can't, " I cried out.

The fucking pervert! This monster was actually going to bring me to orgasm in his weird basement against my will. It was the most horrible thing he could have done. He was going to use my natural proclivities against me for his own sick pleasure. Even just watching Gronk play now made me wetter than the side of a soda can on a hot day, nearly made me come with juicy juiciness. *God, no, please, not here,* I thought. I was so done with it all, so ready to retire from the world of Gronk, but now this crazy über-fan was going to jam it back down my throat.

"W-w-what are you going to do to me?" I whimpered.

"Oh, it'll be good fun! What's wrong with a few dozen orgasms in a row, Leigh? I've been doing it for years now! What is a true fan for?"

"For being nice to women and letting them go home."

"Ha! Funny. She's a funny one."

Chad pressed a few buttons and the chains chaining me to the Machiavellian Barcalounger began to move. My hands began to drag down from above my head. Pins and needles sparkled in my arms as the hands went lower, lower, lower until they stopped... right in front of my vagina.

"There, that's better," Chad said, smiling. "Easy access for when the spirit moves you."

I lost it. "You fucking pervert! Let me go! I beg you, please! I'll knit you a thousand Patriot quilts... Gronk, Wilfork, Gostkowski, Tedy Bruschetta, Ty Law, Andre Tippet, Mosi Tatupu, Steve *gol' dang* Grogan! Please, just don't make me watch Gronk film! Oh, I'll come! I won't be able to stop! Oh! Oh!!!!!"

Oh, the tears! You should have seen my tears!

Chad spun on his heels and walked up to me. The ferocious gleam in his eyes petrified me. I clamped up, muttered a dozen "sorries," and looked down away from his gaze, whimpering like a beaten dog even though I hadn't been beaten yet. But instead of branding me with one his toys, Chad kneeled down in front of me and boldly met my eyes. Then he leaned over and sniffed one of my feet. Just took a long, wistful inhale. Then he trailed the facemask of his helmet up my shin, to my knee and then up my naked, creamy white thigh. The helmet paused in front of my panties for a few tense seconds, a lifetime, my softness aching and afraid, then he crawled up my stomach, then up my chest and between my breasts. Finally, he pressed the forehead of the helmet, cool and hard, against mine. He pressed it hard and I winced, my eyes wide and shaking, my lips trembling, my whole face burning. "Bruschi," he whispered.

"What?" I whispered back.

"Not Bruschetta. Bruschi. Tedy Bruschi."

"Bruschi," I said.

"Bruschi," he said, and began digging his fingers into the flesh of my thighs.

"Bruschi."

"Bruschi."
"Bruschi."
"Bruschi."
"Bruschi."
"Bruschi."
"Bruschi."
"Bruschi."
"Bruschi."
"Bruschi."
"Bruschi."
"Bruschi."
"Bruschi."
"Bruschi."
"Bruschi."
"Bruschi."
"Bruschi."
"Bruschi."
"Bruschi."
"Bruschi."

"*Tedy* Bruschi," I whispered, broken, my thighs in agony, my thighs on the prize.

"That's right, Tedy Bruschi. Good! Okay, back to the mix tape to end all mix tapes!"

Chad leapt away in a weird kind of leg-flinging ballet gesture and landed with a boom on his naked ass on the floor.

I could tell he had already beaten me into submission—felt it deep down where I am the most moist and a lady—and the true torture hadn't even started yet, he'd only brushed me down with a little Bruschi brush.

With a flick of his nefarious remote, the game began.

CHAPTER VII

I'm Not Touching Myself Over That

It was a play of no repute.

The Patriots line up in the same pattern I had witnessed a thousand times. On the other side was a green team I recognized as the Jets. The ball is snapped and the bodies spring into action. The linemen crunch heads, the receivers launch far and wide like bottle-rockets; the Patriot quarterback fakes a quick screen pass to get the DB on his heels and then hands the ball to the running back. A squat troll with the ball like a bag of the king's coin, it looks like the RB is about to squiggle one way, but at the last second, deadlegs and shoots up a hole in the line that is hard to see from the TV side angle. He takes one or two steps before the defense closes in on him. The play ends with a pile of bodies that takes almost 30 seconds to clear away before the game can resume.

The play was on a loop. I watched it unfold before my eyes six or seven times before I realized what was happening...

Chad was down on the floor in front of me, facing the television, sitting Indian style. It started with a few moans. By the fifth loop of the play, he was really getting into it. Moaning, groaning, moaning, groaning, his silver helmet swaying back and forth in the glow of the TV. And...

Fwap, fwap, fwap...

He was masturbating.

Both hands had slid down his front and worked at the tool I could not see. My breath went shallow. My heart raced. *It has begun*, I thought. *Finally, the real-deal fucked up shit is to pop off. Dammit, Dan! What the hell is taking so long?*

I knew Dan was up there in the world, tearing the neighborhood apart, trying to find me. Kidnapped! I was kidnapped right from my own home! It was only a matter of time before Dan stormed this perv-man-cave with a SWAT team and they blasted Chad into a million points of light. I mean, it should have been obvious... Chad had wanted me for so long. He didn't pretend to mince words in public. And I knew Dan wasn't ignorant of history. This story was as old as time. A classic. A jealous man kidnaps the comely lady of his friend and all hell breaks loose. A thousand ships are launched. War. A soldier-filled horse as a gift. Yes, I knew Dan was out there. That kept me sane. All I had to do was to give Chad what he wanted, show a little leg, play for time, and soon enough Dan would come smashing through the door behind me with a SWAT team to the rescue.

But would he be in time?

Chad's arms were really pumping now. His arms were going up really high and then coming down very fast. How big was this penis of his? Soon though, after the umpteenth loop of the play that, frankly, was boring me to tears, a different kind of sound began to weave in with Chad's animal moans of pleasure: Moans of pain.

"Ahhhh," he moaned. Then: "Aiayeeeeee…" A screeching weasel of agony. His wails filled the man cave.

He looked down at his groin and then up at the TV, then down at his groin again. He seemed frustrated at something.

Then I accidentally coughed and fucked up his rhythm. His head flung around with unholy speed. He stared at me. He looked me up and down. He seemed to be surprised at something. Had he forgotten I was there?

"Oh my God. Are you not seeing that?" Chad asked, and there was the fap-fap noise again.

"What?"

"The play."

"Of course. Fifty times."

"How are you not masturbating?"

I smirked. "Are you out of your mind? That's not sexy at all."

"And why is that?"

"It's just a dumb run play. It gets blown up right at the, uh… the, uh…?

"Line of scrimmage."

"Right. Line of scrimmage. If the RB hadn't leaned forward at the end it would've been a loss for a yard. I'm not touching myself over that. Are you nuts?"

The fwapping noise suddenly stopped. Chad stared at me. Rage rose in his face. It went all red. He pressed a button and the loop paused.

"TOUCH YOURSELF NOW, WOMAN!" Chad screamed, "OR I WILL TOUCH YOURSELF FOR YOU!"

"But… that doesn't even make any sense, Chad," I whispered and began to pretend to touch myself for this madman.

Chad gritted his teeth and stood up. He walked over to a glass case full of cleats and smashed his head through it screaming like a wild man of the jungle. Then he fumbled with the remote and suddenly I was jolted with a thousand watts of electricity.

Pzzzzrrrrttttttt!

I screamed out. I was in hell—my bones were razors rattling in my flesh.

The jolting stopped and I gulped for oxygen.

"Watch it AGAIN!" he yelled. "I mean seriously WATCH it." He pressed a couple buttons and the play began again, this time at half speed.

As the play took its predestined course I witnessed with dread Chad's jockstrap raise a bit from the front of his groin. "See!? See that!?" he fumed at me.

"I'm sorry Chad, I'm *so* sorry, what? What is it?"

"This is perhaps one of the greatest Gronkowski plays of *all time*."

"But he didn't score or anything. Is he even playing?"

Chad bent over in laughter. "HA! Not in the play!? Leigh, he IS the play. Watch." The play ended on the TV and began again at half speed. "That's him right there."

It *was* him; I felt a surge in my loins. Oh Chad, you vile tempter. The play happened again and I watched Gronk's massive body at the end of the line, and I quivered with excitement against my will—except this time he didn't fly into the flat or split the seam for a puss-destroying pass. Instead he ran to the left and knocked a defender out of the way for the running back to get by. Hardly something that would get my electric ribbons all ajiggly.

"Okay?" I said when the play was over.

"Of course! It makes so much *sense* now," Chad fumed at maximum volume. "How could I have not seen it before?" he yelled and began to pace back and forth, looking at me through the red facemask of his helmet with boiling eyeballs.

"What is it?" I twinkled, crinkling.

"It makes so much sense. Out on the field at Gillette. The butt of butts. The Gronking to Remember. It makes so much fucking sense now... You're a Touchdown Queen!"

"What the hell is a Touchdown Queen?"

"Oh, oh, this changes things. God DAMMIT this changes things."

I sank into the seat as much as I could. "What? Changes what? What did I do?"

Chad's pacing picked up apace. He was muttering

to himself, fingering his gewgaws, running his palms along the dildos, the paddles, the framed portraits of James Orthwein.

Panic set in again. I had visions of being dumped in a river somewhere, my body naked, or besmirched and burnt up in a piping hot Franklin Stove somewhere remote in a log cabin the woods. Oh, Dan. Where the hell were you already with the rescue team?

"Whelp, there's nothing for it, Mr. Orthwein," Chad said to one of the portraits of James Orthwein on the wall, "Just have to change things up a li'l bit. That's all. Go a little deeper. Deeper than deep…"

CHAPTER VIII
Deep in the Neutral Zone

My training now began in earnest. It was a Training Camp in the truest sense of the word. Forget Two-a-Days, this was an All-Day-Every-Day affair.

"It's a crucial play. It's 3-and-1. If the RB hadn't gotten that one yard, they would've had to've punted. I mean, you know what happens next..."

Chad drew the boring-ass play up on a dry erase board. He'd gone out through the door behind me that I couldn't see and wheeled it in with a blast of artic wind that made me shiver in my panties—made me think maybe we weren't in the basement of his McMansion at all, possibly somewhere far out in the woods.

Also, this: My pussy was barking like a mad dog for heavy petting.

"Instead of punting," Chad continued infuriatingly, "the Pats march down the field and score a score to seal the deal. Talk about teamsmanship. Talk about a team. If Gronk hadn't made it across the line to shank the DE in the scrum, oh, oh what a play... The team effort... oh... yes... the team effort... ungh... is what gets me, oh... Talk about a team... oh, oh, dear yes... team effffffff..."

Chad began to hump the air. His taut, delicious buttocks circled as he scribbled on the board. I was near to bursting. All this deep Gronk stuff was turning me out. Darkness moved across my vision as the X's and O's dug into my very psyche. And my brain felt as if it were receding into a basic place. Who I was before my kidnapping was breaking down. It was a do-over, a rebooting. There was a forest, there was mucus. There was a rage of wanting. Animal lusts began to clog the highways of my synapses. I tried to fight it—was I strong enough to defeat it?

"Why are you doing this to me," I moaned. "Please, no more. Oh God, yes, more. I want more. No! Why, why, why?"

This was pure torture.

"Because there's no 'I' in team," Chad said.

A few hours later we switched to another play.

"Now look at this designed counter. It displays what happens when a team works together. There's no showboating here, no Running Back making a flashy cut, no dazzling footwork to make an agent go *ka-ching!* at the expense of the team. It is all "Do Your Job" and Gronk is what makes it happen. The ball is snapped and Gronk is already in motion. Now, as you can see, the Pats have left the Right Tackle unguarded... here," Chad said, pointing at the TV and then at the dry erase board. "Now, if your nuclear orgasm of a Tight End doesn't make it across the line in time— oh Lord, just look at how my log has lignified thinking about this—or goes deep instead, the play is broken up for a loss and the crowd deflates and the battle is lost and maybe the war. But Gronkowski is a blocking master, he owns the neutral zone, this play is all about football fundamentals, blocking, doing your job, and the game plan against this nickel defense works so... so... oh... mmm... exploits the D... exploits... that... D... No going deep, oh, just going deep, oh... deep in the neutral zone..."

I squirmed in my Barcalounger prison. I had been masturbating for hours now of course, because Chad was focusing all the attention on Gronk, but because there were no touchdowns my delicious touching was coming to nothing. I was rubbing myself absolutely raw. The chains were tight on my wrists, but I had full range to explore myself, sexually. My fingers worked my clit, moved across the line like Gronk in motion to pick up the lead block.

A few hours later we were deep into some other brain-eraser...

"Now, tell me. Should the running back hit the A gap or the B gap?"

"How the hell should I know?"

Chad looked at me coldly. He walked up and took both my nipples in his large, capable hands and twisted. I sunk into the seat, pleasure and pain walloping me, turning me messy and chunky like cottage cheese. "A Gap!" I moaned, "Oh sweet scoundrel, part my two offensive linemen like beef curtains and split my A gap, fleet of foot."

Instead of that, Chad stepped back pressed the remote. The chains holding my ankles pulled tighter and spread my legs even further apart. He looked down at me, licking his lips, "If you want me in there, you need to study tape."

As Chad broke down the game tape, my personality was being broken down as well. The jumble of colors of bodies sank deep into the mud of my person, like a dinosaur falling into a tar pit. I began to understand the power of teamwork. Or rather, the understanding was being drummed into me by a vile tempter.

Teamwork: imagination, finger, clit. A writhing, three person team.

The sex rose up in me, hot and nasty. I needed a nasty fucking. It did not matter from who. Danimal, Chadimal, Gronkimal, Leighimal.

"Why don't you come over here with that magic marker of yours, Chad," I moaned. I was delirious. Who was it that really spoke?

"No. There's no 'I' in team, Leigh. I can tell you're still all about you. This isn't about you. When you tell me what it's all about, I'll let you go, I'll give you everything you want."

"Please!" I moaned and dug my fingers into my dripping wet pussy. It throbbed, it truly throbbed for a mob of linebackers to come in and sit a spell, have some tea-and-fucky-sucky.

But the orgasm would not come. I was not ready yet, this I felt, though it was the one thing I wanted in the whole world.

A few hours later we switched to another play.

"This works for so many reasons, but the most important reason it works is because all the players are working as a team. This isn't the glorious touchdown, this isn't the castle beaming in the clouds, this is the foundation, the muck and the dirt, the cement that holds that castle aloft. What good is a TD—let me put it another way—A TD is *impossible* without all this gruntwork down in the trenches just like Versailles isn't possible without the gruntwork of a million serf-laborers laying the foundation."

"I wish for you to lay my foundation."

"Okay, look. *Get* serious! I'm *serious!* The D is lined up in a 3-4 package. But Belichick and Daniels have dialed up an extra offensive lineman. What do you think that's for?"

"I want you—I need you—to dial me up with your package."

"Incorrect. The extra offensive lineman adds strength and versatility to the running game. Here is another instance where Gronk becomes important."

And again Chad zapped me with a thousand volts of juice. My body shook and shook, I felt the orgasm come close, so close to the line, but it would not turn over. Frustration ravaged me and I screamed out: "Vile, villainous tempter-villain! Vile Chad!" At mention of *dat name*, horny heat sizzled within me like a griddle at a Sizzler, pushing me nearly into the red. I could think of nothing but orgasm, I was so, so, so very close to coming, if only Chad would show me a touchdown video! All these run plays were turning me on, getting me all greasy and sizzly, but seriously blueballing me, as they were not incendiary enough on their own to jazz me up fully. "Please, please, please, show me a score, show me a TD, show me a sexy sixer!"

"Answer me first. Why is there no 'I' in team?"

"How the fuck should I know!?" I screamed. I was seriously out of it. I writhed, squirmed, bucked—I was like a bucking bronco begging to be ridden, like in one of Denver Bronco Peyton Manning and John "Papa John" Schnatter's televised, seething homoerotic *pas de deux*.

"Watch," Chad said and unpaused the game. On the TV the players slammed into one another and I stroked my hot pussy like a porn star. I worked the slot, I really did. I tickled my clit, pinched lightly up and down my lovely lady folds like I was making a pizza crust (Papa Gino's not Papa John's), sunk my fingers deep, deep to the lowest knuckles inside me and still I would not come. I was barely watching the game, but somehow I knew the game was watching me and it turned me on to be watched.

"How the hell is Gronk important to that?" I mumbled, lost in a neutral zone of pleasure and pain.

"He's used as a diversionary tactic. The defense thinks he's gonna fly out into the flat, but instead he helps seal the edge for the running back to gain extra yardage. If the End were able to wiggle out of Gronk's manly grasp, he'd have wrapped up the running back for a loss."

"Oh, oh, God, please wiggle out of my manly grasp for a loss, I beg you! Wiggle out of my manly grasp for a loss!" My brain was humid mush. I was like a cat on a hot tin roof. My pussy barked for implosion. I needed it. I needed a Gronking more gronkatudinal than the world had ever seen. Chad was torturing me. Torturing me with game tape of the most boring plays in NFL history!

A few hours later we switched to another play.

"ARGGHHHHH!!!"

Thus several days were spent in sexual frustration and weirdness as my psyche was turned to mush like a cleat-chewed, soggy field on an unseasonably warm winter's day.

I know, I know... It *was* wrong. It *was* malfeasant... It *was* felonious what Chad was doing to me. He was destroying who I was. But the thing was... and I'm not afraid to admit it now: I think I was beginning to like it.

CHAPTER IX

Two Leighs for Every Chad

Chad put the mental in Football Fundamentals… Blocking. Tackling. Picking up the blitz. Jamming at the line of scrimmage. Creating turnovers. Clock management. All was inserted into my empty brain. I was becoming an encyclopedia of football skills and plays. And with each new tactic, each new drill or formation, my existence became that more inextricably linked to football down in my core, my sexy apple core, my applebottom soul.

For now there was no more Leigh. There was only Leigh. (It appeared the primal, fuckmonster part of me deep down inside germinated from the same gestational molecule that the pain-stakingly jejune librarian and *Stitching-and-Bitching* Leigh came from too. *Anyway*, what I'm getting at is that we were both named Leigh, but we were leagues apart now.)

My pussy throbbed with the fury of ten thousand goats.

And it demanded herding.

"Take me, take me you football God!" I screamed over and over, the lurid eyes of so many Patriots upon me in the framed pictures all over Chadmiral's Quarters. I wanted them to come down off the wall and take me as one in a gangbang of Super Bowl halftime show proportions. The Machiavellian Barcalounger vibrated beneath me like a monolith vibrator—it had many, many uses I discovered, up to and including a built-in toilet and a dildo/butt-plug assembly on a mechanical arm that came up to please whoever sat in it.

Everything was becoming so transparent and *real*. The chair. Football. My naked body chained and bolted down, a slave to the game. That's what it was: I was a *slave* to *football*. And I was so very happy to be a slave to such a sweet game. Oh, you game! Sweetie! A team game! I laughed with joy, I cried with joy. The game is what it was all about. And I had no one to thank for my new beginning except Chad—sweet, sweet Chadmiral.

But still he would not pound his massive cock into me. Chad would not consummate our new love. He would not do me that solid. I remained unsolidified—liquid and gas, ready to conform to a container, but the container would not declare itself. I begged for it. Oh, how I begged for it. I drooled after his jock, his taut buttocks, his rippling abdominals, his biceps that hoisted with manly girth the non-permanent magic marker and the remote control. I moaned and begged for it. But as soon as the game tape was on, I shut my trap up, knowing that the game would eventually draw us closer, as the flue of a Franklin Stove uses an inverted siphon to draw the fire's hot fumes around the baffle.

I also realized with sadness that Chad was no longer masturbating to the game. He seemed to be waiting for me. Or reveling in his role as educator. His cock had long since destroyed his jock support. It was hard constantly—a coat rack waiting for a nice fur coat. The straps hung at his side, the cup nowhere to be seen. Perhaps it was behind the bar somewhere, or in the mysterious cold place on the other side of the doorway behind me. But still his mighty Priapus Chad would not employ.

Was Chad giving me a real-life example of what teamwork was? Did he refuse his carnal release like a desert ascetic knowing that I had not fully flowered yet? That I was not worthy of the plucking? Oh, how I longed to flower.

"Why won't you fuck me!" I screamed at him. The edge of non-climax had grown a hundred yards wide. In that space I lived, a spurned woman.

"You're not ready."

"Why did you bring me here? To what end? Don't you want me? You always said you did. Well, I'm yours for the taking. TAKE ME!!!"

"I will not take you as you are."

I couldn't stop myself. Though I had been broken down into shards of Leigh, the Leigh that had replaced Leigh still contained questions of her creation myth. These questions which gnawed at me I now rifled off at maximum volume: "What is the point of all this? You said you needed me to finish *some* thing. Why? Why do you need me, some chick who knew nothing about football except that it creamed her shorts? Why do you masturbate about football? And why won't you do it now? Why do you have a thick, hard dick right there and refuse to use it? Fuck me, Chad, fuck me or end my life. I cannot stand this torture any more! And what's behind that fucking door that's so fucking cold?"

Chad stood there and listened to my words, a hulking nude Adonis in a shiny silver football helmet with a massive erection prodding the air. When I had finished my diatribe he placed the marker on the little shelf below the dry erase board and walked around Chadmiral's Quarters.

I followed Chad with my eyes. He was deep in thought.

Was this it? Was this the end of the road? Would I live to see another day? Would I have a monster of a 'gasm or nah?

Finally, after much deliberation, his hands behind his back and his long dick out in front of him leading the way like a mine detector, Chad stopped his thoughtful pacing.

He positioned himself in front of me, arms akimbo. I quivered with nerves. It had been days now. With all the humid football training I'd forgotten what nerves was like. But here I was, doing the Jello-fat-guy-walking-by thing again, staring at a cock swaying back and forth in front of me like a snake charmer's flute.

"You can go no further in your training," said Chad with great import.

He leaned closer and put both of his hands on my shoulders. He looked deep into my soul. "Whether or not you're ready, you go no further. In answer to all your questions... I have but one question for you. I will ask you one question and that will determine whether we can proceed, or..." and here he got real dark and arch, "go no further."

"Ask it," I said, defiantly.

"I will show you one more play. Then I will ask you the question. And the answer will decide everything, Leigh. Absolutely everything. My quivering cock demands it. Your life depends on it. But not just yours. My life, the lives of billions of humans now living and yet to live are depending on it. All life everywhere. I haven't been able to explode in a manly way for years now—I've burnt myself out working on the antidote for humanity's ills. But I haven't been able to finish it. I am *so close*. I thought that you would be able to help me. There is a question—a riddle—that I've been unable to unlock. And I've been waiting for "the one," to join me, to help me find the answer. All it takes is one more ejaculation for completion, then my work will be done. The work of a lifetime, Leigh. The saving of all of humanity when the world comes to an end. Little did I realize that you would be so naïve to the ways of football, but I have taught you much, and you have learned much and come so far."

I, nude, nodded my head and Chad played the tape.

CHAPTER X
The Answer of I

Chad's final play is not what I expect at all. And yet I had been expecting it for my entire life.

It is short. Just an extra point play—something so boring that people usually miss it getting snacks from the kitchen.

It's the Patriots' kick. The snap is made. The handle is good. And then the kick... is good. Two referees arms are up. Add another point to the Patriots score, which I see has been a frivolous exercise, because now it's 59 to 24, New England over Indianapolis, in the wee minutes of the fourth quarter.

But then something catches my eye. It's number 87. Gronkalish. He's walking back to the sideline, his arm limp at his side. His teammates surround the field goal kicker, patting him on the head like a three year old at his birthday party, but Gronk is walking back to the sideline. You can call Gronk anything you like, but you can never call him late to a party. I know this play. From my days fingerbanging myself watching Gronk vids online, I know exactly what this play is.

"Well?" Chad says. "What is happening here? Why did Gronk break his arm in this frivolous play?"

Oh God, wait—what? I knew the play, but what was Chad asking me? I start to panic. What was he doing there? Why was he out there? Where was he—

And out of this hectic fury in my brain an answer ushers forth.

A feeling of peace comes over me.

I feel my jiggly ribbons of electric jelly jettisoning to life in my central nervous system...

Yes.

I look Chad deep in his boiling eyeballs.

"He's going deep in the neutral zone. On an extra point attempt. He broke his arm doing it. And he was willing to do it, because there's no 'I' in team."

Chad unleashes a wide, wild grin at me. He is keyed up. "Y-y-yessss!" He begins to stutter. "Y-y-y-y-y-y..." Fumbling with the remote, he presses a few buttons. The chains around my arms unlock. "Why— why— w-w-why..." He put his arms on my shoulders, and I his.

He was really boiling now.

Was I right?

"Am I right?" I asked freakishly, spazzing out. I am jazzed up beyond belief, keyed up from days of torture. The emotion is boiling in both of us.

I feel the eyes of the universe upon us. We are Columbuses. We are Copernicuses. We are Einsteins.

"Why is there no 'I' in team?" Chad shoots at me, almost bereaved. He is crazed. The helmet rattles on his head.

"Because then there wouldn't be a team. There would be 'teami,' or 'teiam,' or 'iteam,' which aren't words."

"Good! Yes! But that is known. Go deeper." We squeeze each other's arms.

"There is no 'I' in team, because there is…"

"Yes?"

"There is…"

"Come on! I know you have it in you, Leigh. Answer the riddle that has plagued humanity for a billion centuries!"

"There's…"

"Bring it!!!"

"There is no 'I' in team, because…"

Chad hummed. His whole body hummed, "Hmmmmmmmmmmm…"

"…there needs to be 'MEAT' in team!"

"Hosanna in the highest!!!"

Instantaneously, both Chad and I have massive, multi-lingual orgasms. Chadmiral's Quarters is filled with the ferocious tribal moaning of two human beings—nay—two ululating, interplanetary fuckmonsters laying eggs across the universe.

The Barcalounger buttplug and dildo deslurp from my scuppers as the scuttling climax storms me perfectly.

White hot soldiers of the apocalypse thunder across my body, swinging battleaxes, firing muskets, lighting off fireworks—my body shakes, quakes and breaks. I jiggle so very jiggly. Chad hasn't pressed any buttons, but my legs fly all over the place so violently they actually snap the chains binding them to the chair.

My legs hurl up into Chad's body with devastating punter-strength and *POW!* he goes flying across the room, eyes closed, smiling the mysterious smile of the Mona Lisa.

In my last micro-mini-moments of consciousness I see Chad mid-air. He has a plastic or maybe glass football in his hands. Where did it come from? I see it is open on the top. His massive cock and gigantic testicles, themselves as big as footballs, unleash a torrent of cum as torrential as I have ever seen. Gallons of his white cum fill up the see-through football as Chad's body Hail Marys across Chadmiral's Quarters...

I lose consciousness, happy.

CHAPTER XI
What is This Beauty Before Me?

Someone could really write a book about that briefest of moments you experience when you wake up but you don't know where you are yet. Even after you open your eyes, when the morning is a question that seeks the answer of the night before, the room confuses, waits for confirmation from memory. There's a whole drama in there, where your conscious comes online, and boots up in the unknown. First, there is awareness of self. Then, surroundings. It would probably sell well (the book) if it were marketed properly.

Well, my surroundings booting up after I came online were confusing as fuck. I opened my eyes onto a big ball of confusion. There was a bar. There were football mementos and sex toys everywhere. In front of me a television the size of a JumboTron plays a loop of an extra kick.

Where was I? Who was I?

Then I recognize the play, the extra kick, and it all came back to me.

Everything.

Here we are in a brave new world, I think to myself.

I am sprawled across the Barcalounger, I am completely naked, my pussy is still throbbing, hot and messy, from the apoplectic orgasm hours before.

I look down and see Chad. He is sitting up now, rubbing the sleep from his eyes. The football filled with his jism is in his lap. It sloshes back and forth. He looks down at it and smiles. Then he looks up at me and smiles. I look at him and smile. Big smiles all around.

Finally after a few minutes of a meeting of the Mutual Smiling Appreciation Association, Chad gets up and comes over to me, the white football in the crook of his bent arm.

"So…" he says.

"I know," I say.

We both laugh gently, knowingly. We've been through a lot together. He reaches out his free hand to me. "Come. I want to show you something."

"What is it?"

"Come on. You've earned it."

I take his outstretched hand and stand up. It's my first time vertical in a long, long time and I wobble. Chad reaches out and catches me. I hold his body close. We hug.

Then he takes me to the door that had been hidden from my view during the whole training session.

Chad opens the door. I look through and all I see is a vast darkness, like the space between stars. A cold blast strikes us, which would have under normal circumstances made me go running for clothes, coat and scarf, but we are still warm from our orgasms hours or days before, like the heat lingering in the ducts of a Franklin Stove long after the last log has gone out.

Hand-in-hand like Adam and Eve, naked and naïve, we walk into the darkness. Chad fumbles with a light switch off to the side.

Suddenly he finds the switch and cold blue neon overhead lights a hundred feet up come to life and illuminate a scene of such... such sublimity I cannot hope to take it all in at once. What I see is incredible: a gigantic room a hundred yards long and fifty yards wide.

"It is... I don't... *understand*," I whisper. "What is it, Chad? Tell me, what is this beauty before me?"

He does not answer right away.

We walk out into the middle of the room, as big as a warehouse and as cold as a meat locker, our exhalations condensing before us. There is even a few inches of snow on the ground.

The room is an indoor football field. And not only that, but it is populated with football players. They are frozen in the middle of a play.

Chad and I stroll through the game like time travelers. It is as if life itself has paused: lifelike linemen butt heads, receivers run routes on the edges of the field, a running back squirts through the neutral zone to the left for a screen pass. I am mesmerized by the detail.

"What are they made of?" I whisper, my voice full of wonder.

We are near what looks like the quarterback.

"Isn't it obvious?" Chad says. He reaches out and touches the player. "Here, taste."

I lean over and lick the arm of a player that looks like he is about to sack the quarterback if he weren't frozen in time. I recognize the taste instantly.

"Semen!" I shout and we both laugh.

"Correct you are, my love."

I look at all the players frozen in the heat of battle. They are all sculpted of the same milky white substance. "Yours?" I ask.

"Yes," Chad responds, demure.

"But what *is* this, Chad?"

"Don't you know?"

"I mean, I can tell it's the Patriots. And who is the other team? Oh, the Raiders. But is there some significance to this particular game or is it from your imagination?"

"Here, maybe this will help you understand."

Chad takes the glass football full of his ejaculate from his arm and holds it out in front of us. With a flick of his wrists, the glass splits down a seam and comes away, leaving a perfectly sculpted regulation NFL football in his hand, except that instead of inflated leather, it is solid all the way through with male spermatozoa. In the brief few minutes that we'd been on the refrigerated field, Chad's jizz had frozen solid and taken the shape of it s container.

"Amazing," I whisper.

Chad takes the ball and places it in the quarterback's hand. I see now that the QB is Tom Brady. His arm is traveling downward, or forward, it is hard to tell, and he is only less than one second away from being hit by gunning, icy, jizzy Raider Charles Woodson, except an eternity will come and go before the tackle actually lands in this frozen display piece.

Then it comes to me. I slap my naked forehead. "Good God, is this the—!"

"Yes."

"Tuck Rule Game?"

Chad smiles and walks away. I follow.

We circle the players, hand in hand, quiet, for some time. I take it all in, entranced by the attention to detail, the magnitude of the history here on display.

"Tell me about this place," I finally ask with what I hope are reverent and respectful tones.

"Do you know of the Terracotta Army of Qin Shi Huang?"

"I don't know. Do I?"

"You probably do. Remember? It's the army of warriors and charioteers some farmers found underground in China in the 70's. It was truly magnificent. It'd been lost for centuries. Over 8,000 sculptures made of terracotta, built to protect the first emperor of China in the afterlife. In a necropolis the size of a football pitch."

"Yes, yes, I've seen pictures of it. Is that what you're doing here? Are you building a mausoleum?" A quick image of death flitted in the back of my head like a black butterfly against a window.

"No, not a mausoleum. For any king or emperor, I mean."

"Oh."

"There is so much talk of Global Warming. And

the speeding up of our climatic cycle. The next Ice Age will be here before we know it, Leigh. When the world ends or a thousand years from now when the world has moved on from the present reality, I want them to discover this room and know what we were like as a people. And to know exactly when and where the greatest football player who ever lived survived his first true test of wills: The January 19th, 2002 AFC Divisional 'Tuck Rule' Game."

I tightened my grip on Chad's arm. It was all so heady, bracing and beautiful.

He continued. "I've built this underground lair to survive a thousand years of climate destruction. It will survive the next ice age. What you masturbate to comes out in the genetic wash, so to speak. And so my seed will populate the next human wave."

"Wow." I was nearly in tears.

"And I owe it all to you, Leigh."

"Really?" I squeaked.

"The gallon of cum was the last amount I needed to make the football. It was the final piece. I had been stymied for years. Unable to ejaculate. It'd been building up, building up, and I'd grown despondent. Viagra, Cialis, none of that stuff worked. Andrea couldn't milk me to fruition. I lived my life hoping, searching for an answer. I desponded. I considered stuffing this place with dynamite and blowing it up... But then along came you. You, Leigh. You. You and your Gronkified bonerosity. It renewed my passion. It returned me to life. *You* were the *real* final piece. You made all this possible."

We had circled back around to where Brady

tucked the ball. I couldn't take it any more. It had been hours and I was hornier than horny again. And I looked down and saw Chad had regained his erection. It was gigantic, nearly twelve inches long and thick and juicy.

Passion had found its way back to us. I felt my neutral zone wetting for a gronking.

"Oh God, how I want you," I moaned. His body was so close—so very close and calling unto me for a hallowed gronking.

"Take me," Chad hummed hotly into my ear.

We crumbled into each other's arms. I pressed my soft little body against Chad's muscular, artist body.

My resolve to remain vertical is overcome. We fall to the snowy pitch, our bodies entwined. We kiss. His tongue fills my mouth and I grab for his hardness. I can barely get my hand around it. Talk about girth.

We roll around like two teenagers. Now Chad is on the bottom, I lay flat on his body. I circle my ass around his groin, trying to match my pussy with the head of his cock. I am so wet now that his dick slides all over my lips, my cheeks, my taint, my neutral zone...

Maybe it was the thought of neutral zone that did it. But in that brief instant before I clenched my tight pussy down on Chad's upright dick I looked up at the door leading to Chadmiral's Quarters—I could see the TV loop of Gronk going deep in the neutral zone.

Only it wasn't that play anymore.

The tape must have gone past that loop. And it was looping an entirely different play now.

Gronk catches a pass, knocks over two defenders,

then a Free Safety and barrels into the end zone.

I know this play too, I think. Actually, I know it very well. All too well…

It is the Gronking to Remember. I watch with growing emotion as Gronk scores a touchdown and there it is: Dan throws me like a ragdoll down underneath the spike and it plows into my body.

There in the Tuck Rule Repository I let out a violent, soul-beaten scream. All that has been taken from me comes roaring back. I am no longer the Chad-created Fuckmonster. I am Leigh who has always been Leigh. I've always been this Leigh.

I look down with horror and disgust at the monster who did all this to me. His eyes are closed, awaiting my pussy to swallow his cock. I am aghast, humiliated, a guilt-ridden mess. What have I become? Where is Dan? Where is Dan? Where is Dan? How could I have done this to my sweet Dan? Oh Danimal, where are you? Why haven't you found me yet?

Quickly, I stand up.

"Y-y-y-you! You! You…" I stutter with anger and the fury of ten thousand goats.

Chad opens his eyes in shock, looks up at me. His eyeballs boil again. Gone is the lust. Suddenly I see the death in his eyes.

He tries to get up. He is going to get up and now I will surely be murdered by this psychotic fan.

I panic. I look around. How do I get out of here? There are no doors except the one leading into the torture chamber.

I panic and reach out for anything I can get my hands on.

"You ungrateful—!" Chad shouts.

I snatch the cum-football out of Brady's hand. It is heavy and slippery like a greased bowling ball but I act fast. I hurl it down straight into Chad's groin as hard as I can.

The cum football explodes into Chad's dick. Crushing into his nuts. His eyes go comically wide and a wintery wheeze croaks from his throat. His legs fold up into his chest. He curls into a ball around his sperm ball like an oyster around a pearl. I know I have only a few moments to find the way out of here before Chad is able to get off the ground.

My mind races, my eyes dart everywhere looking for a doorway out.

An escape! My kingdom for an escape from this castle of weirdness! God, my sweet Lord, please deliver me from this weirdness. I would do anything to get out of here and into the arms of my Daniel once again. Really, it's like a Franklin Stove of weirdness how weird this whole experience has been.

CHAPTER XII
Before the Hat Act of 1732 and After

The man of the house sat before a guttering fire, lumped all around by a dozen quilts in a high-backed chair, miserable with the flu and baffled by a great many things.

It was January. The year, 1742. Winter had been exceedingly harsh. Alas, winters had always been harsh in the Colonies, but lo, these past few periods of hibernal turnover had been wondrously vile to the constitution, and Benjamin had been catching the pip for weeks.

Poor Richard's Almanack was still selling briskly, but for how long would it remain vital? He wasn't ready to retire to Chadds Ford yet. His foray into the German language newspaper market had been an abject failure. (There was a lesson there, he thought, something about a penny lost...) The Junto had recently fallen to fruitless bickering over booklice. Attempts at making spinning wet glass sing had come to nothing. In a word: money was tight before the Hat Act of 1732—now things were looking grim for the coffers.

Indeed, there was much in his mind on which to cogitate. But most of all, though, he ruminated on how cold his ass was and how his wife Deborah was of late not forthcoming with her feminine favors.

How to get my queen to repeal the blockade? he thought and began to weave his hands around in front of his eyes, as if to solve the problem by maneuver of phantasms. A tome of erudite, yet recondite material sat at his side, *Holzsparkunst*, barely pecked at. Undoubtedly, he knew, the march of history had been marked by the battle for resources. Wood was scarce of late, costly. And the American spirit, aye, a true American Patriot spirit, as Franklin, born and raised in Boston knew, was one of efficiency and ingenuity. Only the strong survive, and these days that meant loose musketry. If he were to stave off another war such as *The Seven Years'*, he knew it could only be by bold invention.

Ah, the room has grown cold while I have sat conjuring visions, thought Benjamin. "Wife, more wood for the fire! Deborah!" he called.

"You baffle me, Benjamin," Deborah said coming into their chambers. "We have no money and here you sit, a bump on a birch, feet to the guttering fire. Your bastard bantlings are oozing out from the woodwork like sap, of want of food and education, and wood—wood, you ask? I've a mind to cold pig you. You needst get back to thy grindstone if you want to use *that* wood again, my husband. Methinks this illness is but an art."

She eyed him with matronly disapprobation.

"I have the flu!"

"You baffle me!"

"I have the flu!"

"You baffle me!"

"I have the... *Hold*." Benjamin raised a palm.

"Wife, hand me a feather and parchment!" Benjamin ordered. An idea struck him, just as that bolt of lightning to the rod that one storm-ravaged night when he was flying a kite with his young lover and then somehow discovered electricity?

Deborah did as ordered.

And then, with deft fingers flying over the paper, Franklin sketched his figments, laughing all the while. Deborah knew that look. She smiled in anticipation.

Finally he flourished the parchment. "By artful construction of cast iron *baffle* and *flue*, this new fireplace—I will call it a... a... a "Pennsylvania Stove"—shall heat the same space using half the wood!"

Soon, he bethought himself, *House Franklin will be swimming in a Schuylkill of British Pounds Sterling, and I will be out from under thine cat's foot, woman, floating mine hand up thine hoop skirt, m'lady like cold air up a basement baffle and I owe it all to thee, thy feminine foundations to my masculine manse.*

"This illustration baffles me, my Laird, but if thine calculations are true, the future will reward thee with accolades and the present with remuneration. Huzzah! Truly this is a *Franklin Stove!*"

"And truly, my pet, the most baffling things in the world are the most beautiful," Benjamin said to his better half, reaching for her fastenings. "Now, to bedchambers, you demirep!"

CHAPTER XIII
Freedom Williams

I'm no stranger to engineering history. A climate controlled place like this needs vents. I find the flue to the Tuck Rule Necropolis easily. Really, it's hard to miss. Circling all the way around the room was a type of moat that slunk up behind the back of the wall. How important it is to know things.

Before the sense came back to Chad and his pulverized nuts and he ensnared me once again in his revisionist history where a football game is the pinnacle of human endeavor, I dive under the wall. About twenty feet to my right I see a ladder. I leap at it. Hand over hand, foot over foot, I float upward like forced air.

After a hundred feet I come to a door in the ceiling. There is a simple deadbolt. I unlock it.

In no time at all I am outside. My head comes flying out of an escape hatch and my naked body follows. I fall onto dirt and dead leaves.

It is nighttime and I am in the woods. I see, not far off, the back of Chad and Andrea's house through the backlit trees.

But holy fucking heck! Air! Fresh air! Fresh air and not the fetid recycled fuckwind of the Chadmiral's Quarters & Necropolis. I breath it in joyously like a dog hanging from a speeding car window.

Tears explode from my face like vigorously shaken soda bottles. Oh, sweet, sweet FREEDOM WILLIAMS.

But I am not free. I know this. I won't be free until I am in Daniel's arms and Chad is behind bars drinking toilet wine and ejaculating onto his own face for cigarettes.

I'm naked but I don't give a fuck. Take me as I am. I sprint out of the woods and onto the street. I'm emotionally keyed up so I run down the middle of the road instead of the sidewalk.

Our house is only about a mile from Chad's but I make it there in less than ten minutes, the streetlights and woman's intuition my only guide. This is Suburban America: not one single car passes me the entire time.

"Daniel!" I shout when I get to our driveway.

"Daniel's not home," Chad says. Chad is standing right in the middle of our front yard like a naked psycho lawn jockey. "Why did you leave, Leigh?" he says. "The ball in the balls? Holy shit, that felt *amazeballs*. Like Super Bowl ∞!"

How in the fuck did he get here before me?

79

"No, no, no, no, no!" I scream.

"What?"

"Where is Dan? Did you kill him, you sick fuck?"

"No, he's just not home is all."

"How did you get—how do you get places so fast, you sick fuck?"

"What do you mean? I drove. It took two seconds. I even stopped at the Dunkin Donuts drive-thru on the way. You want this flatbread? Not really hungry as I thought I was."

"Where is he, you sick fuck?"

"Who?"

"Dan!"

"Um, he—he went to um... on vacation?"

"Then why is the light on? I see someone in there—DAN!!!"

"Dan can't hear you, Leigh. Come on, come on back to Chadmiral's Quarters. I'll let you whale me in the dick again—hey!"

I ran to the side of the house.

"Hey wait, don't do that, hey—hey, neutral zone infraction! Hey, um—"

"Tough titties!"

"No, wait, I'm serious, don't look in there. Hey! Don't..."

I went to the side of the house and looked in through the window to the den. The lights were low, but I could just make out the scene. There were candles lit and a log burned in the fireplace. I didn't even know the fireplace worked. I thought it was ornamental.

"What... the heck is this?"

Then I saw Dan.

I couldn't believe my eyes. Dan was only wearing a towel. His body glistened, his hair slicked back from a shower. He held a glass of champagne in each hand as he sauntered into the den.

Sitting on the floor in front of the couch, facing away from me, was a woman. Dan bent down and kissed her. I could only see the back of her head, her frizz of hair backlit by the television. My heart cried out. I was missing—I WAS MISSING—his wife, me, Leigh had been kidnapped. And here he was with another woman. Not out looking for me, not tearing the neighborhood apart, not launching a thousand ships, not doing anything to save me whatsoever. My heart shrank to a pea in my chest.

I couldn't believe it. I was numbed dumb with senselessness and insensibility.

Then I looked at the TV.

"Football? They're watching football..." I whispered to Chad. "I'm *missing* and he's watching football with some *slut*."

"I know. It's not even football season."

"I just... don't..."

"Oh my..."

"What?"

"...God."

"What, Chad—*what?*"

"That's the 2010 Divisional Playoff game."

"Yeah?

"When the Jets beat a far superior Pats team at Gillette to get to the AFC Championship Game. Are you seeing what I said now? About Dan and the

Jets?"

Though I am now powered by 1.23 Jigawatts of football knowledge as a result of Chad's debauched crash course, his football chatter lands on deaf ears. I am too distracted by what I see in the room.

The scene gets hot very quickly. The windows even abruptly fog up, but just before the view fades to gray completely, I see the blurry slut woman take off Dan's towel and push him onto the floor. His dick is already erect and sproi-oi-oings back and forth. They kiss. She grips his tool. He caresses the arcs of her hips. She runs her slut hands through his wet hair. Dan swigs from his champagne glass, spills some down her breasts and proceeds to lick it off. She straddles him and they begin to make love, reverse cowgirl style, both facing the television. She rides up and down on his dick while they watch a football game on TV.

I...

This I cannot bear.

I can't even; I sprint around to the back of the house to the patio off the den. Chad chases after me, whisper-yelling: "Leigh, no, Leigh, come back, wait...!"

From the patio I can hear their voices. "Fuck yeah... fuck yeah... fuck yeah, Sanchez... oh Sanchez, oh dirty, dirty Sanchez... Oh God, Dan, yes. I'm riding you, I'm riding your dick so hard... Your dick is *yuge*, Dan, fuck me with your *yuge* cock..."

I fling the patio door open and burst into the room.

My sweet eyes, why do you do what you do when

you do it?

I can't believe my burning eyes.

There on the floor in front of the TV, bare-assed naked as the day they were born and moaning with candied sexual delight, Terry Gross was jumping up and down on Dan's dong.

CHAPTER XIV
A Job Done Wrong

"Sanchize! Ooh, Sanchize!" Dan moaned hotly into Terry's ear.

"Oh! Oh!" Terry shouted in ecstasy, bouncing up and down like a kid on a wooden pony. "Your thang is yuge, Dan... *Yuge!*"

I stormed into the room.

"What the fuck?" I screamed, annihilating the sexy mood. "Terry Gross? What—? I don't—"

Terry leapt off Dan's thang and stopped, dropped and rolled onto the floor like she was on fire. She covered herself up in one of Dan's old Jets jerseys and stared at me, utter hatred in her eyes.

Dan too stared at me. He did not try to cover himself up, just sat eyeballing me with his erection swinging back and forth across his lap like a metronome.

Tick-tock… Dick-dock… Tick-tock… Dick-dock…

Here we were.

Evil was in Dan's eyes. Baleful, hay bales of hate in his eyes.

Naturally, I began to cry. I was immobile, imprisoned by air, locked in the center of the room. I wanted to run to Dan, but his look kept me away. My heart was being ripped in two.

"Dan, what the hell? I thought you said you got rid of her?" Terry suddenly said, Goo Gone-ing the invisible Shoe Goo gluing the room with tension.

"Got rid of?" I squeaked.

"Dunno. Chad, care to answer that?"

Chad entered the den quietly through the patio door. He was naked too. All four of us were naked. Four naked corners of a Love Square.

"I'm sorry, Dan. I know we had a deal, but she escaped," Chad said.

"Nine days later? What the fuck were you doing with her for nine days?"

"What do you care, Jets fan," Chad said "And *you*. Terry Gross. Lady Tee. Queen Tee. You should be ashamed of yourself. You're from Philadelphia for chrissakes. The Jets? Really?"

Terry snarled at Chad.

"Can someone please tell me WHAT THE FUCK IS GOING ON???" I screamed.

"Can't you see, Leigh? I'm a Jets fan. A Jets fan for life! J-E-T-S! I bleed Hunter Green! Pantone 626 C!"

"What? I thought you said you changed—I

mean… What? *I don't care* about that, Dan, I don't care! I just want you! I just want you!"

"It's too late for that, Leigh. You made your decision out on the field at Gillette Stadium."

"That was *all you!* Dan, *you* did that to me! You made me Gronk! I never asked for any of this!"

"But you liked it! You decided to make a career out of it! Throw it in my face every Goddamned day! Every Goddamned day I wake up and there's a new Gronk quilt, a new set of needlework Gronk placemats on the dining room table, a new book signing for *Wife Spiked By Life* to go to at some shitty used bookstore! Fuck it! Fuck it all the hell, Leigh!"

"I don't understand."

"Nobody says you have to," Terry said and pulled out a gun.

I crossed my arms across my body, ashamed of my nudity for the first time since coming into the room. Guns shame us all. "What the—?"

"As you should know, Leigh, when you spike a Gronk in someone's zone place, it's a special thing," Dan said.

"When you Gronk, you Gronk for life," Terry said.

"You mean… you two?" I asked.

"Yes. On the stage at the 92nd Street Y. Us. It *happened to us*," Dan said.

"B-b-but…"

"That's right," Terry said. "In the butt."

"Man cannot live on free breadsticks from Olive Garden alone, Leigh," Dan said. "There has to be free salad too. Terry is my free salad… You bitch."

"I don't get it. So you tried to get rid of me?"

"Tried to. Chad and I had a deal. Made it up on the landing at his house that night of the party. He wanted you, I wanted you gone. An ideal situation. So I drugged you up and dropped you off in the woods behind his house."

"What happens when an unstoppable Chad meets an immovable Dan?" Chad said, giggling.

"Shut the fuck up, Chad!" Terry barked.

"Oh my God…" I whispered. "It was you. Dan… it was *you*. You were the face in the dark that night!" I began backing up towards the door. I had to get out. I had to get free.

"Hold it!" Terry shouted, leveling the gun at me.

"But I couldn't do it, Dan," Chad said. "Leigh was too sweet. I mean not just a Pats fan, but she is like, a football genius. She could coach a team with what she knows, I'm telling you. Forget about the Tuck Rule Necrop—"

"I don't give a shit about that! Chad, we had a deal and you broke it. Now you both have to go. Classically, if you want a job done right, you have to do it yourself."

Dan reached over and took the gun from Terry. He pointed it at me.

"What? No. Dan, take me. But please, the world needs Leigh," Chad pleaded.

"Terry and I'll be rollerblading on your graves while you two both are eating bags of Patriot dicks in hell!"

Terry guffawed balefully. Dan pointed the gun at me and fired. The blast filled the den with its deafening sharp scream.

I flung my arms in front of me, trying to catch the bullet. Next thing I knew there was a huge white mass of naked flesh blocking my vision like a side of beef, like the meat in team.

"NO!!!!!!!!" Chad dove sideways across me, like he was trying to block a field goal. He grunted; there was an ugly thud. His body hit the floor, lolling at my feet.

"Noooo!" I screamed. A demon possessed me. I charged Dan, my arms flailing. The gun flew out of his hand onto the floor near Terry. I saw her pick it up.

"Get her... grunt... ungh... off me... Terry..."

"Get outta the way!" Terry was screaming. "Get outta the way!"

"You coward! Jets! Coward! Jets fuck!" I screamed, clawing at Dan's face, kicking him, punching him.

Suddenly, there were sirens in the distance.

"Shoot her!" Dan screamed at Terry.

But Terry was listening to the sirens. "Is that...?"

Through all this, Chad was trying to speak. "I— I — I called... the police... before..." he was trying to say, "Before I came in..." A flatbread sandwich and a cell phone fell from his limp hand onto the floor. It looked like an Egg White Veggie on Multigrain, but it was hard to tell in the candlelight.

"We've got to move fast!" Dan yelled.

A hundred things happened at once. Before I knew what was happening, Dan had the black bag and the chloroformed rag in his hand. The rag was against my mouth. Terry and Dan were on top of me.

"...burn this place to the..." "...go, go, go..." "...pin it on her..." "...come on, come on..." were the cryptic and meaningful phrases I heard in the last wee seconds before losing consciousness completely.

Darkness.

CHAPTER XV

Deep in the Neutral Zone 2:
My Absolute Hero

I awake in the sweet neutral zone of the micro-moment before opening my eyes to the world. Everything is as it should be. Dan and I are in bed—our warm bed surrounds us. In another minute or so I will open my eyes, stretch, roll over and spoon my Danimal.

But then I actually open my eyes... and it is a punch-drunk *horror*.

I am in an ambulance.

There is something in my throat. I can't breathe.

"I can't breathe!" I try to say and sit up. The lights are insanely bright. Neon bursts into my eyes.

Two EMT's attend me. There is also a policeman.

"Relax, sit back... *Rela*xxxx," the EMT says like

Aaron Rogers, except she is a serious and strong-looking woman, with the wizened face of a sailor, blonde, in her late 40s.

"W-w-what... happened..." I manage to croak out. "Where is Dan? Where is Chad? Where is Terry?"

"Please, there's been an accident, you're okay now," the blonde EMT says. I sit up and look out the window of the ambulance.

"My house is on fire!" I scream.

Then I realize police lights and the lights of fire trucks are whirring across the ambulance. I look out the back doors and see firemen doing battle with the flames. Police are all about too.

A policeman comes to the back of the ambulance and motions for the other one to come out. They speak in quiet, municipal tones on the street and then both come back into the ambulance.

The men in blue look down at me with unhappy eyes.

"What? What is it? Oh, God! Oh, God, what is it," I yell, my voice cracked. "Are they dead? Is Chad gone? They killed him! They killed him!"

One of the policemen lifts my right hand, swabs it, takes note of something. He nods to the other policeman. "GSR," he says.

"What's that? GSR... What's that mean?"

The blonde EMT exhales through her nose, eyes me. "Gunshot Residue," she says like she's seen it a thousand times on the open sea.

"But I—"

The second policeman handcuffs me to the gurney, bears himself up and begins to recite those terrible and foreboding lines: "You have the right to remain silent... etc."

My mind goes blank. What the hell is this? Dan and Terry must have put the gun in my hand, shot it and then set the house on fire. Framed! Those two villains... they framed me!

"I've been framed!" I plead my case to the assembled jury in the ambulance, my voice hoarse, apparently from smoke inhalation.

"EMT's, will you two please exit the ambulance," one of the officers says.

"That's not procedure," the blonde EMT says.

"Need to question the suspect."

"Suspect?" I croak.

"That's not procedure," she says again.

"Get the fuck out of here or there will be procedures for your impeding an investigation!" he shouts.

Begrudgingly, the EMT's go. The first officer shuts the doors after them.

"Please tell me what is going on," I beg them. "Is Chad alive?"

"No, ma'am," says one of the officers. "Whoever or whatever this Chad is comprised of, no, it is not now alive."

"Huh?"

They shut off the lights.

"Wait, what's going on?"

Their eyes glow green.

"Wait, what are you doing? What is that? Is that a needle? What the hell?"

The two policemen descend upon me. I buck, try

to scream. But their hands are on my mouth. One holds me down. The other has a hypodermic needle. He holds it up, backlit by the window of the ambulance, red and blue lights morph and refract through the glass tube.

"Shhhhh…" one of them says. "Just one little itty bitty pin prick and it will allllll be over…"

I scream into the policeman's hand. I can't believe this is happening. The needle comes down on my arm, sharp and ghastly…

Suddenly the back doors fly open. A huge male body is there, filling the entire doorway. Another police officer. He's as big as a monster.

"Get the fuck outta here," one of my assailants barks at him. "We have this."

"No. You don't," the monster speaks. Do I recognize that voice?

The monster flies into the ambulance. A violent scuffle ensues. Bodies in the dark. Quickly, the monster takes care of them, veritably: he throws them out of the club. His gigantic muscles pound into their bodies, slams their heads against the walls of the ambulance.

I don't know whether to scream or just drop dead from fright. I have been through so much.

Then all is quiet. The monster kneels down next to me in the darkness.

"Please…" I whisper, "don't hurt me…"

His arms move across my body. This is it: this is my death.

But then the monster finds my hand that is cuffed to the gurney. With the flick of his wrist the handcuff snaps in two.

"Better?" the monster asks.

"Who are you? I know you," I say.

The monster reaches down to his belt and turns on a flashlight, but keeps it face down into his leg. A scant light illuminates the ambulance.

In the tiny light I see that it is no monster.

"Gronk!" I shout and throw my arms around him.

"Hi, Leigh."

"Wait. You're a policeman too? In addition to being a devastating receiver and a brutal blocker, the complete Tight End package?" I ask, wiping tears from my eyes.

"Ha! No, not really. It's just a costume. But we've been keeping an eye on you ever since The Gronking to Remember."

"Who? The Pats?"

"No, no, more powerful than the Patriots."

"Impossible!" I say.

Gronk laughs. "Look, there's no time. You have to go. You have to escape. I got here just in time to stop these two. More will be coming."

"Who? What? Who are these two? Aren't they police?"

"Not even."

Gronk gets up and peeks out the window. "Shoot! You gotta go you gotta go you gotta go!"

"Go where?"

"The woods. The forest. The trees. Anywhere in America. Just go. Be free and hide somewhere. Anywhere. Get away from all this and you will be safe. Just always know that I'll be with you," Gronk quickly says as he helps me up from the gurney.

"Really?" My body is sore all over, but I can move. I only have on a hospital gown, open at the back. My skin prickles. Was I getting turned on?

"Of course. Hey, when you Gronk, you Gronk for life, right?"

"So you're coming with me?"

"What? No. In *spirit*, Leigh. I'll always be with you in *spirit*."

"Oh."

"Look, more agents are coming. Go!"

"Um, oh, I'm scared!"

"Look. The government and the police may not know it, but I know you're innocent. That's the most important thing. We've known about Chad's work for years, been kept abreast of it. Highly creative, but thoroughly frivolous and besides the point. And of course Dan and Terry were easy to spot. I'm surprised you didn't see it. But it'll all blow over in time. These two, though," pointing at the two policemen he'd dispatched like a couple of practice squad safeties. "We didn't think they'd get here so fast."

"Agents for what? Who's we?"

"There's no time to explain! Just go!"

Gronk flings the doors open. Night air and light and sound blast inward. Two more police officers, or perhaps secret agents of some nefarious foreign entity, leap at Gronk, eyes ablaze with green light.

"Go!" Gronk shouts as he tackles them, my hero. My absolute hero.

That's exactly what I do. I go... I scamper out from the ambulance and make for the woods.

I go, away from the light and the smoke and the chaos and the fame. I run, deep into the dark, wet woods where I cannot be found—the woods between houses like the dark, unknown matter between galaxies.

I escape. I just go. I go deep. Deep, deep into the neutral zone of America.

The End

CHAD GOES DEEP

ABOUT THE AUTHOR

Well, let me tell you about good ol' Lacey Noonan. Lacey lives on the east coast with her kinks, perversions and obsessions. And possibly a husband or two.

When not sailing, sampling fine whiskeys or making veggie tacos, or sailing on a whiskey sea in a taco sailboat, you can find her reading and writing steamy, strange, silly, psychological and sexy stories.

During the day, she is a web designer and web developer.

Twitter
https://twitter.com/laceynoonan

Email
laceynoonan123@gmail.com

Made in the USA
Middletown, DE
06 December 2017